Tio

Lily

Medwen

Shadow

# Fairy
# Unicorns

## Treasure Quest

Zanna Davidson

Illustrated by Nuno Alexandre Vieira

# Meet the Unicorns

Zoe

Astra

Sorrel

Unicorn King

# Contents

Chapter One      7

Chapter Two      25

Chapter Three      39

Chapter Four      54

Chapter Five      70

Chapter Six      85

Chapter Seven      96

# Chapter One

Zoe tiptoed down the garden path. Above
her, the faint curve of a new moon hung in
the inky night sky, casting a glow of
silvery light. Great Aunt May's house was
already shrouded in darkness, while up
ahead Zoe could just make out the Great
Oak – the magical oak tree that led to
Unicorn Island.

Zoe had been to Unicorn Island many times before – whenever she visited her great aunt's house – but this time felt different. For in her hand she held a magical cage of vines, and inside the cage was Shadow – a tiny fairy pony. He had nearly destroyed Unicorn Island and when he'd finally been stopped, the Unicorn King had shrunk him down and trapped him inside this cage. Zoe had been watching over Shadow ever since, but now the King had decided he was no longer a threat, and the time had come to set him free. Zoe could only hope the King was right.

At the foot of the Great Oak, Zoe reached for her tiny pouch of magic dust. Then, sprinkling it over herself, she chanted the words of a spell:

Let me pass into the magic tree,
Where fairy unicorns fly wild and free.
Show me the trail of sparkling light,
To Unicorn Island, shining bright.

At first, she felt a tingling in her fingers and her toes. Then it spread to her whole body, and all at once the world around her seemed to be growing and growing, while she was shrinking, shrinking...all the way down to fairy-size. Shadow, too, had shrunk, and now they were both small enough to pass into the tunnel between the roots. Zoe ran on, down the soft, sandy path, gripping the magical cage of vines.

As she rounded the corner, she could see the glimmering, magical light of Unicorn Island, and then she burst out of the tunnel and into the Silvery Glade.

Zoe gave a gasp of delight. Around her were fresh spring leaves, in every colour of the rainbow, and woodland flowers dotting the banks and paths. She looked down at Shadow for a moment. "Just to think," she said, "you tried to destroy all of this."

But Shadow said nothing, merely glowering at her through half-closed eyes. A moment later, Zoe heard the sound of hoofbeats on the woodland floor, and Astra was galloping towards her. The little unicorn's coat was gleaming, her horn shining, the stars on her coat lit up in the dappled sunlight.

"You're back!" said Astra, smiling.

"I am," said Zoe, grinning in return, before reaching forward to give Astra a welcoming hug. "And this time I've brought Shadow with me, just as the King asked."

She heard Astra's sharp intake of breath as she looked at Shadow.

"Is it unsettling, seeing Shadow again?" Zoe asked.

Astra nodded in reply.

"I was thinking," Zoe went on, "how beautiful it is here, and how close Shadow came to destroying it all. I love how different it is to my world. Everything here seems to shine and sparkle – even the flowers."

"Why not take some back with you?" laughed Astra. "There are so many – you could pick just a few."

"Oh, but they'll wilt," said Zoe, sadly. "Wait! I know!" she added. "I could press them when I get home, and then I'll always have something to remind me of Unicorn Island, even when I can't come here."

She placed Shadow's cage on the ground for a moment while she picked a few of the flowers and popped them into her bag.

"And now," said Astra, when Zoe was done, "it's time to take Shadow to the Unicorn King."

Astra bent down and Zoe swung herself onto her back.

"Are you ready?" asked Astra.

"I'm always ready to fly with you!" Zoe replied. She clutched the cage with one hand and clung to Astra with the other, as the little unicorn began galloping through the Silvery Glade.

Once they'd left the last of the trees behind them, Astra spread her wings and took flight, until they were soaring across Unicorn Island. Zoe drank it all in – the gentle curve of Moon River, the scented breeze floating up from the Flower Meadows

and the magical, weightless feeling of flying
through the airy blue.

Astra swept through the skies and it
wasn't long before the Unicorn King's Castle
came into view, carved from the rock face, its
lofty turrets peeping out through the lush,
tangled vines.

They landed on the little bridge that led
to the castle entrance. Zoe swung herself
down and together they walked up to the
gates. Astra pulled the bell and the doors
swung open to reveal a beautiful, cobbled
courtyard, filled with sweet-smelling flowers.
As usual, it was bustling with fairy unicorns,
all going about their daily tasks, but they
stopped and stared when they saw the cage
in Zoe's hand.

Everyone stepped back at the sight of
Shadow – even though he was tiny and
caged. No one had forgotten him – or the
fear he'd inspired.

"The King is in the Throne Room with the
Guardians," said Astra, as they crossed the
courtyard. "I know because my mother left
this morning to join them. Everyone's

worried about Shadow coming back and I
think the King wanted to reassure them."

Zoe nodded in reply. The Guardians were
among the most powerful and magical
unicorns, who helped the King protect
the island. Astra's mother, Sorrel, was
Guardian of the Woods and Trees.

When they reached the Throne Room, Zoe saw that nearly all of the Guardians had come to the meeting. There was Lily, Guardian of the Flowers; Medwen, Guardian of the Spells; Eirra, Guardian of the Clouds; and Nimbus, Guardian of the Snow; along with Sorrel, smiling at Zoe in welcome.

"Ah, Zoe," said the King when he saw her. "Thank you for coming and for bringing back Shadow as I asked."

Zoe walked slowly towards him, holding out the cage. Some of her anxiety about Shadow faded as she looked into the King's eyes, sensing his strength and wisdom.

"Please," said the King, "place the cage on the ground, then take a step back."

He turned to the Guardians. "I know

many of you are unsure about releasing Shadow, but it is the right thing to do. He no longer has his powers. We have recovered the Grimoire, our most powerful spell book, thanks to Astra and Zoe – and so Shadow poses little threat to us now. It would be wrong to keep him caged forever. We can't do that to him."

The Guardians nodded in reluctant agreement, and the King waited until everyone had moved away. Then he lowered his head, so that his golden horn touched the cage. He muttered a spell, his voice low and resonant, and at once the bars of the cage dissolved into the air.

Then there was a fizzing and a crackling followed by a loud BANG! Zoe blinked as a flash of light lit the room. When she opened her eyes again, there stood Shadow, tall and proud, tossing his silky mane.

At once, the Guardians moved together, horns lowered, waiting tensely for what he might do next.

"Calm yourselves," muttered Shadow. "I have no powers...remember?"

"That may well be true," said the King, "but we cannot trust you after all you've done. You can still plot and plan, we have no doubt of that. So until you win back our trust, we are sending you to an island, far beyond these shores."

Shadow glared at the King, but said nothing.

"Magus, one of our wisest unicorns, has offered to watch over you," added the King.

As he spoke, Magus stepped forward into the room. He was older than the Guardians, with a thick, grey mane, threaded through with silver. But there was a sense of power about him too.

"It will be an honour to protect Unicorn Island," he said, his voice low and gravelly.

"Will you go peacefully?" the King asked Shadow.

"Of course," Shadow replied, standing very still. "Anything is better than that *cage*." He didn't lower his head or make any apology as he spoke, but looked the King straight in the eye.

Zoe could sense that even with Magus taking Shadow away, the Guardians were still unhappy about his release. As the King and Magus led Shadow from the room, they turned to each other and began to talk among themselves.

"I still don't trust Shadow," said Lily. "Not for a moment."

"Nor do I," sighed Nimbus. "I wish he hadn't come back."

"But what choice did we have?" asked Sorrel. "It would be wrong to keep Shadow locked up forever."

Zoe longed to stay and listen, but she could see Astra, beckoning her away.

Silently, Zoe slipped from the room, following Astra as she led her up turret stairs and along marble corridors, until they came to the castle library.

"I've got a plan!" said Astra, her eyes alight. "To make sure we really are safe from Shadow. Are you ready for another amazing adventure, Zoe?"

# Chapter Two

"Oh Astra!" said Zoe. "I should have known you had a plan in mind! What is it?"

Astra opened the door to the castle library. "Let me explain," she said, as they went inside. "You see, I've been worried ever since I heard that Shadow was coming back. What if he could still threaten our island? And then I remembered the legend of the

Silver Chalice!"

"The Silver Chalice?" repeated Zoe.

"Yes!" said Astra. "All little unicorns are told stories about the Chalice. It's a magical object that's been lost for centuries. It's said that if you fill the Chalice with water, and look into it, then you can see the future."

"It sounds amazing," said Zoe.

"I know!" interjected Astra. "So if we find the Chalice, we can give it to the King, and then he'll know once and for all if Shadow really is a threat to the island."

"That sounds great," said Zoe. "But if the Chalice has been lost for centuries, how are we ever going to find it?"

At that, Astra's eyes lit up even more.

"Well..." she said, dropping her voice to a

whisper, "I've been searching the castle library, just to see if I could find out anything more about the Chalice, and I came across a book. It was hidden in the wall of the library!"

Zoe looked puzzled, and Astra led her to an old, faded tapestry, hanging on the library wall. "Take a look behind it!"

Zoe lifted the material, and there, set back in the wall, was a tiny little door.

"Wow!" said Zoe. "Is it...a secret cupboard?"

Astra nodded. "I discovered it one day when the wind was blowing at the tapestry, and I suddenly had an urge to look and see if there was anything behind it."

As she spoke, she went over to the little door and chanted a spell beneath her breath. At once, it swung open.

"I can't tell you how many goes it took to open it!" said Astra, grinning. "It's a very intricate spell. Now," she went on, "take a look inside..."

Zoe reached in and there, right at the back of the cupboard, was a very old, and very dusty book. In glimmering gold writing on the cover it said: Magical Objects of Unicorn Island.

"Can you put it on the reading table?" asked Astra. Then she tapped the book with her horn and the pages began to turn...

# The Silver Chalice

This is one of Unicorn Island's most precious treasures. It is an incredibly magical object, that has helped save the island in the past.

If you fill the Chalice with water and look into it, then you will see a vision of your future.

The Chalice is kept hidden deep underground, in the Treasure Maze beneath Unicorn Castle.

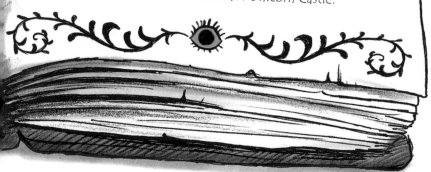

"And there's more," added Astra, turning the page. "Here it says that to find the

Chalice, you have to pass through the Treasure Maze, made up of three rooms. Each room is a test. In the first room, you must answer a riddle. To leave the second room and reach the third, you must take nothing with you, no matter *how* tempting. To find the Chalice in the third room, you must solve the maze."

"Doesn't that sound exciting?" said Astra. "And what's more, if we find the Chalice, we're not just helping the King. I'll be one step closer to becoming a Guardian!"

Zoe smiled at her friend. She hadn't
forgotten what the King had told Astra
– that she had enough powerful magic to
become a Guardian – but in order to prove
herself, she had to do three things to help the
island, and in ways that showed exceptional
magic. On Zoe's last visit, they had found the
Grimoire together, the island's most magical
spell book. Now Astra only had two tasks
left to complete.

"Finding this Chalice is a perfect
challenge," Astra went on. "It looks as if it
will need exceptional magic, and we'll be
helping the island if we bring the Chalice
back to the King."

"You're right," said Zoe, but she still felt
hesitant. "I'm just not sure why this book was

hidden...and why no one has thought to look for the Chalice before?"

"I don't know why it was hidden, but I'm sure it doesn't *mean* anything," said Astra. "And maybe no one's looked for the Chalice as they weren't able to find the book or undo the spell? Or perhaps it's just been forgotten. All the fairy unicorns must have thought the Chalice was lost, or no more than a legend."

"Okay..." said Zoe. "Next question! *How* are we going to find the Chalice?"

"Well," said Astra, studying the book, "there's a little map here. It shows that the Treasure Maze can be reached through a door in the castle – we just need to go down to the cellars and then find the right door."

"I still don't like the sound of this," said

Zoe, peering down at the book. "Remember how the Grimoire was guarded by a Sea Dragon? What's the Silver Chalice going to be guarded by? A three-headed dog? A terrifying snake? A giant cockroach?"

Astra chuckled. "Zoe, you're worrying about nothing," she said. "Look at the book – there's no mention of anything guarding the Chalice."

"Hmm," said Zoe.

"Well, we'll find out soon, won't we?" said Astra, smiling.

Zoe sighed, but she was smiling too. Astra knew her so well. However crazy this plan sounded, Zoe couldn't resist another adventure. And she knew there was no stopping Astra now. The best thing she could do would be to go with Astra and help her.

"What do you think?" asked Astra.

"I'll come with you," said Zoe, with a reluctant grin. "Somebody has to!"

Astra gave a twirl of delight and tucked the book under a pile on the table.

"Let's go now then!" she said. "We'll have to be as quiet as possible. We don't want anyone to notice what we're up to... especially the Guardians!"

But no sooner had they left the library than they bumped straight into Medwen, Guardian of the Spells, and his young apprentice, Tio.

"Zoe!" said Tio, when he saw her, his face beaming. "I heard you were back! Where are you two off to?"

"Nowhere," said Zoe, quickly, then wished she'd thought of something better to say. "I mean...the castle kitchens first. Astra's, er, feeling hungry."

Medwen took no notice. He was clearly deep in his own thoughts, but Tio looked at them both suspiciously.

"But I'll catch up with you soon," said Zoe, as they hurried on their way.

Astra waited until they were going down the castle stairs before she spoke again. "That was close," she said. "I hope we don't bump into anyone else. I really don't want my mother or the other Guardians to find out what we're up to. They'd be sure to stop us."

As they tiptoed past the Throne Room, they could hear the rest of the Guardians, deep in discussion still. Not one of them turned as they slipped by the door. Zoe gave Astra the thumbs up and they carried on, through the courtyard, then down more turret stairs, deeper and deeper until they were in the very bowels of the castle.

When they reached the lowest floor, they saw a long, dark corridor, with rooms leading away on either side. Slowly, warily, Zoe and Astra made their way across the dusty flagstones, looking for the door they'd seen in the picture.

"It's spooky down here, isn't it?" said Astra.

"Definitely!" agreed Zoe, brushing away yet another cobweb. "I get the feeling no one has been down here for years."

She could see old spell books in messy piles, gathering dust, and beautiful, ornate candlesticks on the windowsills, shrouded in cobwebs. When she peered into the rooms, she saw some were full of dried herbs, while others stored ancient banqueting tables and faded silk rugs. Then, at last, at the very end of the corridor, they came to a small door.

"This is it!" breathed Astra. "This is the door that matches the one in the book. This is where the Treasure Maze begins!"

# Chapter Three

Zoe looked at Astra and then reached forward, pushing at the door...but it wouldn't budge.

"It's not opening!" said Zoe.

"Don't worry," said Astra. "I'll try casting a spell. Hopefully a simple one will do it." She thought for a moment, and then began to chant, her voice steady and assured.

Hear my voice, do as I say,

Open now and open wide.

We come in peace, there is no need

To hide whatever lies inside...

On Astra's words, the door swung
noiselessly open, to reveal a dark tunnel
beyond. They stepped through and the door
shut behind them, as if closed by an invisible
hand. Zoe couldn't help a silent shudder.
Even though the castle was just on the other
side of the door, it felt as if they had entered
another world.

Astra muttered another spell beneath her
breath, and a moment later, light shone from
her horn, showing the way. With Astra in
front, they walked down the tunnel, having

to stoop as it became smaller and narrower
the further they went. Then, all of a sudden,
the tunnel opened out into a little chamber,
empty except for a door at the other end. As
they came up to it, Zoe
could see it had a
wooden knocker,
carved in the shape
of a unicorn's head.

And behind them, in
the darkness, came the
sound of footsteps.

"Oh no!" whispered Zoe.
"Do you think we're being followed?"

"I don't know," said Astra. "Maybe it's one
of the Guardians and they've found out what
we're up to? And there's nowhere to hide!"

"Or it could be a terrifying creature that lives down here?" said Zoe, her imagination running wild.

They huddled together, watching, as a shadowy shape emerged at the other end of the chamber. It came closer and closer, and in the glow of Astra's horn they saw...

"*Tio!*" Zoe cried in relief. "I'm so glad it's you! What are you doing here?"

"And how did you know we were here?" asked Astra.

"Well, you left quite a strong clue by leaving THAT book on the table, under my spell books. And it was left open on the page about the Silver Chalice!"

"So I did!" said Astra, sighing. "Sorry, Zoe... I should have hidden it better." Then she turned back to Tio. "Does Medwen know we're here?"

"No," replied Tio, shaking his head. "I didn't tell him, so you wouldn't get into trouble. I decided to come and get you myself."

"We're not turning back, Tio!" said Astra, staunchly.

"You have to," insisted Tio. "That book was locked in a secret place for good reason – to stop any unicorn finding it. You may not know this, but most of the objects in that book carry *a curse*. It's not safe to go and look for them."

"Oh," said Astra, frowning. "The thing is, I don't want to turn back, not unless I really *have* to. What is the curse?"

Tio looked down at his hooves. "I don't know," he mumbled.

"You don't know?" said Astra.

"No, I don't," Tio replied, sounding defiant now. "But that doesn't mean the curse doesn't exist."

"I'm sorry, Tio," said Astra, her voice quiet but firm. "But I'm not turning round for that.

You can come with us, or go back, but I'm carrying on. What about you, Zoe?"

"I'll go with you," said Zoe, knowing Astra would go alone if she had to. "We've started this quest, and I think we should finish it. It sounds to me as if the Chalice could truly help the King."

Tio sighed. "Is there nothing I can say to persuade you?"

Both Zoe and Astra shook their heads.

"Well, I can't leave you," said Tio. "I can't believe this is happening... I've ended up on yet another dangerous mission with you."

He rolled his eyes as Astra grinned.

"Fantastic," she said, turning her attention back to the door. "Now, this must be the first room, which means we have to solve a riddle to pass through it."

"I know that!" said Tio, importantly.
"I read the book too!"

"But what *is* the riddle?" asked Zoe.
"How do we find out what it is?"

"Maybe we should try knocking on the
door?" suggested Tio.

Astra lifted her hoof and rapped on the
door. Zoe gasped as the carved unicorn
head blinked open its eyes.

*"Riddle-me, riddle-me, riddle-me-ree!"* it
said, staring at them all. "Can you answer
these riddles three?"

"Three?" repeated Zoe. "It didn't mention
that in the book."

Tio just shrugged. "I'm hoping you can't

answer them. Then that'll be the end of our quest. That would suit me just fine. I can go back to my library, have a nice cup of tea, and maybe a biscuit or two..."

Astra glared at him.

"Go on," Zoe said to the door. "Tell us the first riddle."

"What goes up but never comes down?" asked the door.

"A ladder?" said Tio, wondering aloud. "A chimney..."

"All those things go up *and* down," said Zoe, gently. "We did riddles at school once, and the answer doesn't have to be an object. Oh! I know!" she said suddenly. "The answer is age, isn't it? It must be!"

"Correct," replied the unicorn door. It sounded unmistakably grumpy that Zoe had got it so easily.

"Oh, well done, Zoe," said Astra, smiling at her.

"The next one is harder," said the door. "The more I take, the more I leave behind... What am I?"

"Well, it's definitely not cake," said Tio, looking puzzled.

"Oh dear," said Zoe. "This one *is* harder."

They were all silent for a while, trying hard to think. The unicorn door rolled its eyes. "What a shame," it said, sarcastically. "You've come for the Chalice, haven't you? And you can't even get past the first room."

"We haven't given up yet," retorted Astra. "And what's more, you don't have a very helpful attitude."

"It's not my place to be helpful," said the door, loftily, "just to read out the riddles–"

"Oh wait! Wait!" interrupted Zoe. "I know

this one too. It's footsteps."

The unicorn door smirked. "No, it's not."

"Are you sure?" asked Zoe. "I was certain I'd got it right."

"Well you're wrong," said the door. "The answer isn't footsteps. Not here, at any rate. And if you can't answer this riddle, you can't pass to the next room."

"Hang on," said Astra. "What do you mean 'not here'? Aha!" she went on, her face lighting up. "The answer is hoofsteps, isn't it?"

"Yes," said the door, begrudgingly. "Well, I've saved the hardest riddle for last. You'll never get this one... I can only live where there is light, but if the light shines on me, I die. What am I?"

"Oh dear," said Zoe, after a while. "I can't even begin to work this one out. Astra?"

But Astra shook her head. "I can't think what it could be either. My mind's gone completely blank. Oh no. We're going to fail at the first hurdle..."

The unicorn door was looking tremendously pleased by this idea. "Most fail," it said. "Few have made it to the second room, in all the centuries I've been here. Although I have to say, I haven't had any visitors in a long time. I'd also like to mention you can't come back and try again. This is your one chance."

Just then, Zoe caught Tio's eye. "Oh, you know the answer, don't you!" she cried. "I can see by your expression. *Please* tell us what it is, Tio."

"Oh Tio, you must," added Astra, pleadingly.

"Fine," said Tio. "The answer is a shadow."

"Correct!" sighed the door. "I never would have thought you three had it in you. Now enter...if you *dare*. And one more thing – once you have passed through the first door, you only have an hour to make it through the second room, and through the maze to the Chalice and back again. After that, the door to these three chambers will be sealed shut to you. TIGHT SHUT! Forever!"

The unicorn door glanced down and they

followed its gaze to see an hourglass, on a little table, which swung itself upside down. At once, the sand inside began to trickle down. "When the sand runs out," said the unicorn door, "you'll know your time is up."

And with those words, the door creaked open...

# Chapter Four

Zoe picked up the hourglass and placed it carefully in her bag, making sure it stayed upright. "Here goes!" she said. "We'd better hurry. We don't know how long it'll take us to get through the maze."

And they all three stepped into the tunnel beyond. This one was much wider than before, but had the same damp, eerie feel.

It had a musty scent, too, as if no one had been this way for years.

"I don't like this," said Tio, trotting along beside Astra and Zoe. "They could really do with some lighting down here..."

But then, as the tunnel began to curve round, they saw the walls were covered with a strange glow, made up of shadowy, flickering colours.

"Somehow," said Tio, "this is even more creepy. Where is that light coming from?"

"It must be coming from the next chamber," said Zoe. "The one we can only pass through if we don't take anything, however tempting," she added, remembering the words from the book.

"Well, that doesn't sound too difficult,"

said Tio, his voice full of relief. And he strode ahead, rounding the corner. "Here we go! I can see the next chamber," he called.

"Wait," Astra called. "Tio! Stop!"

But it was too late. Tio had gone.

"What is it?" asked Zoe, for Astra had stopped in her tracks.

"I don't have a good feeling about this," said Astra. "There must be something in that room powerful enough to tempt a unicorn. I'm hoping it won't affect you, but I'm worried I won't be strong enough to pass through. Will you blindfold me, Zoe, so I can't see?"

"Are you sure?" asked Zoe.

Astra nodded.

Zoe took off her scarf and wrapped it

around Astra's eyes.
Then, placing her
hand on Astra's
mane, she
guided her
down the last
of the tunnel.

The strange, flickering colours grew
more and more intense, the closer they came
to the next chamber. And as they rounded
the corner, Zoe had to shield her eyes from
the glow. They were standing in a room
filled with jewels – more jewels than Zoe
had ever seen in her life. Emeralds,
diamonds, rubies, sapphires – all gleaming
brightly. They filled the shelves, littered the
floor, tumbled out of treasure chests and lay

nestled in nooks and crannies.

And there, in the centre of the room, was Tio, gazing at the jewels in wonder, his eyes transfixed.

"What is it?" asked Astra, her eyes still blindfolded. "What's in the room?"

"Jewels," Zoe replied. "Jewels everywhere!"

"Oh no!" said Astra. "Tio! Whatever you're doing – stop!"

But even as Astra called to him, Tio didn't turn around. Instead, he began picking up the jewels and stuffing them into his saddlebags.

"Tio!" said Zoe. "What are you doing? We can't take anything from this room, remember?"

But Tio didn't even look at her. He just carried on filling his saddlebags, as if enchanted.

"What's going on?" Zoe asked Astra. "Why is he taking the jewels?"

"Jewels are a fairy unicorn's greatest weakness," Astra replied. "That's why we don't have any on Unicorn Island. Gold and silver are fine – but diamonds, rubies, sapphires, emeralds...we find them incredibly hard to resist. But I think we're in more trouble than that... When I was little, I was told the story of the Silver Chalice, but there was another legend too...of an enchanted chamber, full of jewels, that no fairy unicorn would ever have the strength to leave behind!"

"Wait here," said Zoe, tightening the scarf around Astra's eyes. "Let me see what I can do to help Tio."

She hurried over to him and began by talking to him, first gently, then urgently, begging him to stop, just to look at her, but his eyes were glazed and it was as if he couldn't even hear her.

"Nothing's working," she said to Astra. "Is there a spell you can say?"

"It'll take me a while to work one out," Astra said. "And by then, we might have run out of time and we'll *never* get to the Chalice. I don't think we have a choice but to leave

Tio here. Then we can find the Chalice and come back for him. You remember what the door said – this is our one chance."

"That's true," said Zoe, but she still sounded hesitant.

"I'm sure Tio will be safe here," Astra went on. "And we have to get that Chalice, Zoe. It's the only way to find out if Shadow really is still a threat to Unicorn Island."

Zoe took a deep breath. "Okay," she said. "Let's keep going."

With a last glance at Tio, they approached the door at the end of the second room. This time, it swung open before them, without any need for a spell. They walked through it, and down a third tunnel. Only when they had rounded a corner, and the glow of jewels had

faded to darkness, did Zoe take off Astra's
blindfold and place it in her bag.

"Are you ready?" said Zoe, looking ahead.
"Because now it's time for the maze..."

Ahead of them lay a vast underground
cavern. The maze itself was made out of
thick walls, hewn from the black rock
around them, and lit with flaming torches.

"We don't want to get
lost," said Zoe, checking
the hourglass as she spoke.
"We must leave enough
time to get back again
and help Tio."

"We'll leave a trail
for ourselves," said Astra. And as Zoe
climbed onto her back, she muttered a spell.

Then Astra began moving through the
maze, as fast as she could go in the dim light,
leaving a trail of shimmering stars in their
wake. It wasn't long before they came to
their first turning.

"Which way now?" Zoe wondered aloud.

"I've been reading about mazes ever since I
found out about the Chalice," Astra replied.
"The important thing is not to double back

on yourself. Let's turn left here and then
make sure we always take a new path."

"Good plan," said Zoe. She knew she was
placing all her trust in Astra, but her friend
had never let her down before.

They headed deeper and deeper into the
maze, always taking a new path, until they
came to a junction where both turnings were
lit with stars.

"What do we do now?" asked Zoe. "We don't want to end up going in circles."

"It's fine," said Astra, her voice sounding so calm and determined that Zoe felt proud to be her friend. "I remember this too. We can take the same path again, but never more than twice. I'll light this one in a different colour so we'll know we've done it again."

On and on they went, taking turn after turn. All the time, Zoe could feel the cold dark pressing in on them, the weight of the castle above and the black rocks all around.

"I don't like it down here," said Astra.

"Nor do I," agreed Zoe. "I really hope we're nearly there."

Astra kept trotting down the narrow passageways, this way and that, making sure she never took the same path more than twice.

Zoe kept checking the hourglass. "It's already over half-way and we don't know what might happen and there's Tio to fetch. We can't risk being stuck down here..."

"I know," said Astra. "But I'm going as fast as I can."

Zoe tried not to worry, but she found her gaze fixed on the hourglass, watching the sand trickle away. "I'm starting to feel nervous," she admitted. "We really are going to have to turn back soon. Only two more turns, Astra, it's not worth the risk."

"Okay," said Astra.

Zoe could hear the reluctance in her voice, and really hoped she was going to be able to persuade Astra to turn back.

Astra took one more turn...and nothing, just another passageway. And then, at the end of that, another turn...leading to yet another passageway.

"Please, Astra..." said Zoe.

"Just one more turn," said Astra, "I've got a sort of feeling."

And without waiting for Zoe to refuse, she rushed forward, almost skidding around the

corner...and there, at last, was the centre of
the maze. Before them lay a great circle
carved out of the rock, with passageways
running off in all directions and, in the
middle, raised up on a plinth, was the Silver
Chalice, shining in the darkness.

# Chapter Five

For a moment, both Astra and Zoe just stood there, staring at the Chalice, as if they couldn't quite believe they'd really found it.

Then Zoe reached over and gave her friend a hug. "At last!" she said. "Well done, Astra. Your plan worked."

Astra looked back at her, smiling. "I wasn't sure we'd ever get here...but we did it! Thank you for sticking with me, Zoe."

They both went up to the Chalice, peering over the edge. "Look!" said Zoe. "It's already full of water."

"Shall we try it now?" asked Astra. "I know we want it for the King, but it's so tempting, just to have a little peek ourselves."

Zoe glanced down at the hourglass. "We can if we're really quick," she said, "and we should be much quicker going back, as we can follow our trail. You go first, Astra."

Zoe stepped away from the plinth, to give her friend some space, and Astra bent her head over the Chalice.

For a moment, all was still, then a silvery mist floated up and out of the water, surrounding Astra in magical wraith-like

wisps. Zoe could sense that strong magic was
at work.

Astra stayed very quiet, her eyes locked on
the water, gazing intently at whatever the
shimmering image was revealing to her.

"Well?" asked Zoe, as soon as the mist had
cleared. "What did you see? Did it show you
your future?"

But Astra just stood there looking pale, shocked, a deep confusion in her eyes...

She opened her mouth, as if to say something, but then she seemed to stop herself. "I didn't see anything," Astra said, in a quiet voice. "Perhaps the Chalice isn't magic after all...and that's why no one's bothered coming to get it."

"Are you sure?" asked Zoe. "It definitely looked as if there were something happening. There was this glowing mist..."

But Zoe stopped as Astra hung her head, refusing to meet her eye.

"There was nothing, really," Astra insisted. "Why don't you try?" she added, stepping away from the plinth.

Feeling uncertain now, as if something

strange was going on, Zoe stepped up to look. The water glimmered in the light of the flaming torches and she felt herself enveloped in the same swirling, glittering mist that had wrapped itself around Astra. It was as if she and the Chalice were cocooned in their own little world. At first, she saw nothing, not even her own reflection, but then the water in the Chalice cleared and she could see someone that looked like her, but all grown up. "My future self!" gasped Zoe.

She looked happy. She was sitting at a table, and writing. At once, Zoe knew what that meant – she was going to be a writer when she grew up! Her heart began to beat with excitement. But then she noticed that

there was no sign of Astra. And when Zoe
thought about Unicorn Island, the waters
turned dark and empty. She didn't know
how she knew, but she realized at once what
the Chalice was trying to tell her – that
when she was older, she wouldn't be able to
come back to Unicorn Island.

Zoe stepped away from the Chalice,
feeling incredibly sad.

"Well?" asked Astra, tentatively. "Did you see anything?"

Zoe couldn't face telling her the truth. She wasn't really ready to believe it herself. "I was all grown up," she said, "and I was writing. Maybe that means that one day I'll be a writer."

Astra nodded, but stayed strangely silent.

"We'd better hurry back now," said Zoe. And she reached for the Chalice, her hands resting on the handles.

"Let's go," agreed Astra, "although I think I feel differently about the Chalice now. Maybe it's not such a good thing, to be able to see the future?"

"Maybe not," said Zoe. "Let's just hope it can help the King." She lifted the Chalice from the plinth, but the moment it was in her hands, there was a great rumbling and shuddering all around.

"Oh no!" said Zoe. "What's happening?"

"I don't know," replied Astra, as the cave continued to shake. "Uh oh...this doesn't look good!" she added, as a jagged line snaked its way across the floor.

"The cave – it's cracking open!" cried Zoe.

The walls shook too, and rocks began tumbling down the sides. The whole cavern reverberated with the sound.

"It's not just cracking open," said Astra, looking up as great chunks of the roof plummeted to the floor. "It's falling in!"

"Tio was right all along," said Zoe. "The Chalice is cursed!"

"Hurry!" said Astra. "Jump on my back!"

Zoe swung herself up, still holding the Chalice, the water sloshing over the sides. Then Astra was off like a shot, galloping back through the maze, rocks tumbling down around them.

"Thank goodness we left a trail," said Zoe, as the path of glittering stars led them through the darkness.

Zoe clung on tight as Astra twisted and turned. The journey seemed to take forever and all she could hear was the BOOM! BOOM! of rock crashing onto rock. Once, she looked over her shoulder, only to see the maze walls collapsing behind them... If they took a wrong turn, they might never be able to find their way out again.

"It's okay," said Astra, at last, her breath coming in fast pants. "We're going to make it... The end is in sight."

And to her relief, Zoe saw the end of the maze, and beyond it, the passage that led to the jewel room.

But at that moment, there was a great crash as another rock landed right behind

them, inches from Astra's hooves.

Astra bolted forward, taking the last part of the maze at a leap, and landed with a skid in the tunnel.

There was one more giant rumble and a huge boulder slammed down at the entrance to the passageway, blocking off the maze for good. They had only just made it in time.

"Well," said Astra, with a wobbly smile. "You were right. It was much quicker on the way back!"

Zoe gave a shaky laugh. "Much quicker," she agreed. "I only hope *this* tunnel isn't going to start collapsing too!"

"I think we're safe here," said Astra. "Before, I could sense the magic of the maze falling in on itself – it felt like a powerful curse at work. But that's behind us now."

"Well thank goodness for that," said Zoe. "Let's go and get Tio – and get out of here – before those doors are sealed shut!"

Astra nodded and cantered the last part of the passage. "I can't wait for fresh air again," she said.

As soon as they reached the jewel room,

Zoe slid from Astra's back. Putting down the Chalice, she hurried over to Tio. His saddlebags were bulging with jewels and he was still trying to stuff yet more diamonds inside them. "Come on, Tio. We have to leave while we still can. You can take some jewels with you, but we must go."

Tio, however, took no notice, but carried on stuffing his saddlebags.

"What are we going to do?" said Zoe. "We can't leave without him! But if we don't find a way to move Tio, we could be stuck down here forever. Nobody even knows we're here!"

She took a deep breath, trying to calm her rising sense of panic. "Astra, what shall we do? We could try pushing him out of the room? Or maybe it's time to work out that spell, to break the hold the jewels have on him?"

But that was when she realized...

In their rush to escape the maze, she'd forgotten to blindfold Astra again. And now, like Tio, she too was gazing at the jewels, utterly transfixed.

# Chapter Six

Zoe ran over to Astra. "No! Don't do this!"
she said. "Not you, too." She put her arms
around Astra's neck and called her name.
But just like Tio, it was as if Astra couldn't
see or hear her any more. She had fallen
under the spell of the jewels.

Zoe looked over at the door and thought
about trying to run for help, but she knew

she wouldn't have enough time before the hourglass ran out – and then what if Astra and Tio could never get out?

In desperation, she tried pushing Astra and Tio towards the door, but she didn't have the strength to move them.

"There must be a way to break the enchantment," Zoe told herself. "If only I had something that could call them out of their trance. What could it be?"

All of a sudden, she remembered the golden bell in her bag. It had been a gift from the Unicorn King, and he'd told her that all she had to do was ring it, wherever she was, and he would come to her. But even as she reached for it, she realized now was not the time to use it. If the King came here, he too would see the jewels, and then he might fall under their spell as well. She couldn't risk it.

But there, next to the bell, were the flowers she had picked from the Silvery Glade. She knew the glade was Astra's favourite place on the island – it was where she lived with her mother. Could they

somehow have the power to break her
trance? Without holding out much hope,
Zoe wafted the flowers under Astra's nose,

hoping to remind her of
the world she loved.
At first,
nothing
happened. But
then Astra's
nostrils began to
twitch. And as

she breathed in the scent of the flowers, Zoe
could see the light flooding back into her
eyes...and then the recognition.

"What happened?" asked Astra, her voice
dreamy, as if she were only slowly coming
back to herself.

"It's the jewels," Zoe explained. "We forgot to blindfold you...and they had you under some kind of trance. These flowers broke the spell. Are you okay? I'm going to try them on Tio now."

Astra nodded, still a little dazed, and Zoe looked down at the hourglass again. "We're nearly out of time," she said. "I really hope this works."

She hurried over to Tio and held the flowers by his nostrils, just as she'd done with Astra. But, this time, nothing happened.

"It's not working," said Zoe. "What are we going to do?"

"I'll find a way," said Astra. She strode over to Tio and began to chant spell after spell, until the air was sparkling with her magic. But nothing was working, and Zoe could see that Astra was starting to tire. Her voice was growing weaker; the stars on her coat, that always lit up with her magic, were growing duller.

"Oh, Astra," said Zoe, catching sight of the trickle of sand in the hourglass.

Astra looked over at Zoe, a hint of desperation in her eyes. "I'm not leaving Tio down here," she said.

"No," agreed Zoe, "I won't either," although she couldn't help a lurch of fear as she said those words. "Let's try to think. Why did the flowers work on you, but not on Tio? Is it just that he's been here longer, so the spell is harder to break?"

Astra didn't reply at first, and Zoe could

see she was deep in thought.

"Perhaps," Astra said, "the only thing that breaks the spell is something you really love. For me, it's the Silvery Glade, but what is it for Tio? What is the thing he loves most?"

"If it's a place, then it's definitely the castle library," said Zoe. "Could you conjure up an image of it?"

Sorrowfully, Astra shook her head. "There's something about this place that seems to be sapping my magic. I'm exhausted," she went on. "I need to build up my strength again. But I know we don't have time for that…"

Zoe went over to her. "Don't give up, Astra," she said. "Think of how you coped all those years before you knew you had magic inside you. You always find a way – even without magic."

"You're right!" said Astra, and her eyes were shining now. "I've got an idea. Maybe a spell book would work. After all, books are what Tio really loves! He always carries one with him."

She hurried over to him and began nosing around in his saddlebags, jewels spilling out as she searched.

Unnervingly, Tio just stayed gazing blankly at a jewel in the cave wall.

"I've got a book!" said Astra, triumphantly. Then she walked round to face Tio, holding the book close to him, willing it to work.

Breathing in the scent of the old book, Tio gave a slow start, as if waking from a deep

sleep. Then he shook himself, and looked around in confusion.

"Where am I?" he asked. "Zoe? What's going on?"

"It was the jewels," explained Zoe. "They enchanted you, but Astra found a way to break the spell."

"Now, quick," said Astra. "We haven't much time. Empty your saddlebags, Tio, and then we can leave. They'll weigh you down otherwise. We must hurry!"

"Oh crikey," said Tio, looking like his usual flustered self now. He began tipping out the jewels as fast as he could, which fell with a clatter to the floor.

Then Zoe grabbed the Chalice and they all raced out of the jewel room together, pushing open the door to the riddle room, just as the last few grains of sand were trickling through the hourglass.

"We've got seconds to go!" cried Zoe. "And the last door is shut. Quick, one of you, cast a spell to open that door!"

"Oh dear, oh dear..." said the carved unicorn head, looking very pleased with itself. "Took too long, did you?"

"Ignore it!" said Zoe. "We can do this!"

Tio looked over at Astra and saw how drained she was. "I'll do it!" he said. And he began to chant...

Hear my voice, do as I say,
Open now and open *fast!*
Do not keep us *from* our home,
We leave *in* peace, so let us pass.

The door swung open, as the last grain of sand dropped to the bottom of the hourglass. With relief, all three of them stumbled through and collapsed, exhausted, in the dank cellars of Unicorn Castle.

# Chapter Seven

Tio was the first to speak. "When will I learn to stop going on adventures with you two!"

"At least we've got the Chalice!" said Zoe. "Come on! Let's take it to the King. Tio, do you mind if I put it in your saddlebag?"

"Go right ahead," said Tio. "Turns out the Chalice wasn't cursed after all!"

Zoe and Astra exchanged glances. They

would have
to tell Tio
about the
collapsing
cavern later.
But for now,
they wound
their way up
and out of the
cellars, until

at last they reached the castle courtyard.

"I'm so happy to have the sun on my face

again," said Astra.

"Me too!" said Zoe, smiling at her. Then

she turned to one of the unicorns passing

through. "Do you know where the King

might be?" she asked.

"He was last seen heading to the library," the unicorn replied.

"Thank you!" said Zoe. She grinned at Astra and Tio. "Nearly there!" she said.

When they reached the library, Zoe saw the King, with Medwen beside him. They

were standing over the book of Magical Objects of Unicorn Island.

The King looked up as they came in, his face flooding with relief. "I'm so glad you're here," he said. "We saw the book and worried you'd gone in search of the Cursed Chalice."

"The Cursed Chalice?" said Zoe. "Is that what it's known as?"

"Yes," replied Medwen. "That's why this book is kept hidden! So no one is tempted to go looking for it. It's said to be hidden deep under the castle but throughout history, whoever has gone looking for it, has never returned... In fact most of the objects in that book are cursed, one way or another."

"Exactly what I said," Tio pointed out, looking at Astra. "You never listen to me!"

"Well, the Chalice was only a *little* bit cursed," retorted Astra.

"What do you mean?" said the King.

In reply, Zoe reached into Tio's saddlebag and brought out the Chalice. "Well," she said, "as a matter of fact we *did* go looking for it."

The King and Medwen stared at the Chalice in shock.

"I think we'd better explain," said Astra.

"I think you better had," replied the King.

So Astra told them everything – how she wanted to find the Chalice, so they could find out if Shadow was still a threat, and as a way for her to complete another challenge on her way to becoming a Guardian. She told them how she stumbled across the book, how Tio joined them, everything it took to find the Chalice...and then escape again.

"I didn't believe Tio when he said it was cursed," said Astra. "And I should have done. But at least we have it now."

Zoe placed it on the table in front of the King.

"I hope it helps the island," said Astra. "But I know I've failed in my task to become a Guardian. I didn't use any exceptional magic. And when I tried to save Tio with my spells...I couldn't."

"You haven't failed," said the King, gently. "You worked as a team to solve the riddle, you made it through the maze, and most important of all, you didn't abandon Tio.

You refused to leave without him. And if that's not exceptional, I don't know what is."

"Thank you," said Astra, her voice almost a whisper, a faint blush under her pale coat. "But I couldn't have done it without Zoe."

"That's what makes you so special," said the King, "the way you work together." Then he stopped and looked at the Chalice. "I'll take this to my room now, and study it. You were right, Astra – this Chalice will help me know if Shadow still poses a threat. But it's important to remember that no future is set in stone. Now, you only have one more task to go before becoming a Guardian. That is quite a feat."

The King smiled at them all, then left the room with Medwen.

"Congratulations!" Tio said to Astra. "And I might not have said it before...but thank you for rescuing me, and not leaving me down there, on my own, in the darkness..." He gave a shudder at the memory.

"Thank you for coming with us, Tio," said Zoe, hugging him. "And now," she added, "I think it's time for me to go home."

Together, Zoe and Astra walked through the castle. When they reached the little bridge that arched over the waterfall, Zoe climbed onto Astra's back once more. Then they flew over Unicorn Island, all the way to the Silvery Glade, both lost in their own thoughts.

As Astra set her down by the Great Oak, Zoe wanted to tell her about what she'd seen in the Chalice. It seemed wrong, somehow, to keep it a secret. But before she could put her thoughts into words, Astra spoke.

"I did see something in the Chalice," she said. "I didn't tell you straightaway as I've been trying to work out what it means."

"Go on," said Zoe.

Astra took a deep breath. "I saw myself wearing a crown," she said. "And not just any crown – it looked like the crown the King wears. And I knew, I just *knew* when I saw myself, that I wasn't simply trying on the crown. The Chalice was telling me that one day I would be the Unicorn Queen, and that I would rule over Unicorn Island." She stopped and looked up. "What do you think it means, Zoe? I was too scared to ask the King. I've been telling myself that maybe the Chalice just shows you the future you want to see – the one you secretly dream of?"

But Zoe shook her head. "No, it doesn't Astra. I didn't tell you the whole truth either. I didn't just see myself as a writer... I was on my own...and just like you I knew what the Chalice was telling me...that as a grown-up, I wouldn't be able to come back here. We wouldn't see each other any more. And that isn't something I'd ever wish for. So the Chalice really must be showing us the future. Maybe that means you'll be the Queen one day? And that's not a bad thing!"

"But that's not all," said Astra, her voice dropping to a whisper. "In the Chalice I wasn't much older than I am now. I've been thinking – does that mean something is going to happen to the King?"

"Don't worry about the King," said Zoe, smiling. "He can look after himself. He's the wisest unicorn I know. All we can do is wait and see."

"And enjoy the time we have!" said Astra, smiling back at her. "After all, it's a long time until you're a grown-up! That's years and years away! Remember what the King said, too – no future is set in stone. I'm sure there's a magic that means we can always be together."

"I really hope so," said Zoe. "And I'll be back soon," she added, as she turned to go, "for our next great adventure..."

Enter the world of the

# Fairy Unicorns

and collect every
enchanting tale

**Coming soon...**

## Islands in the Sky   ISBN: 9781801310352

Zoe and Astra are on a new quest to help the
Unicorn King. This time, their adventures lead them
high into the sky, in search of the Floating Islands.
But someone is following them and the islands
are not all that they seem.

Will Zoe and Astra be able to complete the quest
and help the King, or have they taken on more
than they bargained for?

Designed by Brenda Cole

Edited by Lesley Sims

With thanks to Alison Kelly

First published in 2022 by Usborne Publishing Ltd., Usborne House,
83-85 Saffron Hill, London EC1N 8RT, England. usborne.com
Copyright © 2022 Usborne Publishing Ltd.